Amazing Cats and Dogs

Pamela Rushby

Contents

Cats, Dogs and Humans 2
The Forgotten Prince's Cat 4
Félicette – The First Cat in Space 8
The Grumpiest Cat on the Internet 12
Ernest Hemingway's Polydactyl Cats 14
Royal Dogs 18
Two Loyal Dogs 22
Lassie – The Dogs Behind the Star 28
Glossary 31
Index 32

Cats, Dogs and Humans

Cats and dogs have been living with humans for many thousands of years. No one is sure exactly how long, but it could be anywhere between 15 000 and 30 000 years ago that cats, dogs and humans first interacted with each other.

Today's cats are **descendants** of the African wildcat. The long-ago **ancestor** of dogs is the grey wolf.

The African wildcat is also called the Egyptian wildcat.

Many thousands of years ago, wild cats and dogs were probably attracted to human campsites by the food scraps that humans threw away. Then, as many humans moved from being **nomadic** hunters and gatherers to being farmers, the wild cats and dogs came close to their villages to hunt the rodents and other small animals that fed on crops. The wild cats and dogs gradually became tamer.

The grey wolf is also known as the timber wolf, and is the largest wild dog.

Over time, humans discovered they could put cats and dogs to work. Cats caught mice and rats. Dogs could be trained to hunt or to herd domestic animals.

Today, some cats and dogs are still kept as working animals. Others are kept purely for pleasure as much-loved pets. And from ancient Egypt to the space age, some cats and dogs have done amazing things.

The singer Taylor Swift carries one of her much-loved cats.

This artwork from the thirteenth century shows King John of England chasing a stag with a pack of hunting dogs.

The Forgotten Prince's Cat

Thutmose (pronounced *thoot-moh-suh*) was a prince of ancient Egypt. He was the oldest son of the **pharaoh** Amenhotep III and Queen Tiye, and he lived around 3500 years ago. He never became pharaoh himself, and his life was almost forgotten. So, how do we know about him now? Mainly from the **sarcophagus** of a cat – his pet cat, Ta-miu.

This small statue shows Prince Thutmose grinding grain for bread, and is one of very few representations we have of him.

Prince Thutmose was clearly very fond of Ta-miu, whose name means “the female cat”. When she died, her body was mummified and placed in a sarcophagus made of limestone. The sarcophagus was covered with carved pictures and **hieroglyphs**.

One picture shows Ta-miu sitting in front of a table piled with food; these were special treats that Ta-miu would be able to enjoy in the **afterlife.** On the back of the sarcophagus is a picture of Ta-miu with a lotus flower, a symbol of rebirth. This meant that Prince Thutmose hoped that his beloved pet cat would live again in the beautiful and happy afterlife.

Carvings on Ta-miu’s sarcophagus show her sitting at a table full of food, while the goddess Bastet stands behind her.

The lid of Ta-miu's sarcophagus is covered with hieroglyphs, and these include Prince Thutmose's full royal titles, "Crown Prince, Overseer of the Priests of Upper and Lower Egypt, High Priest of Ptah in Memphis". So, it is known that at the time Ta-miu died, her **grieving** royal owner was the crown prince, the eldest son of the pharaoh.

But very little more is known about Prince Thutmose. His name disappears from history, and his younger brother became the pharaoh Akhenaten. It is assumed Thutmose died young.

Cats were **sacred** to ancient Egyptians, who believed them to be a form of their cat-headed goddess, Bastet.

This small bronze and gold statue of the goddess Bastet was made in Memphis in ancient Egypt.

Almost nothing would have been known about Prince Thutmose if it were not for the sarcophagus of his pet cat, Ta-miu.

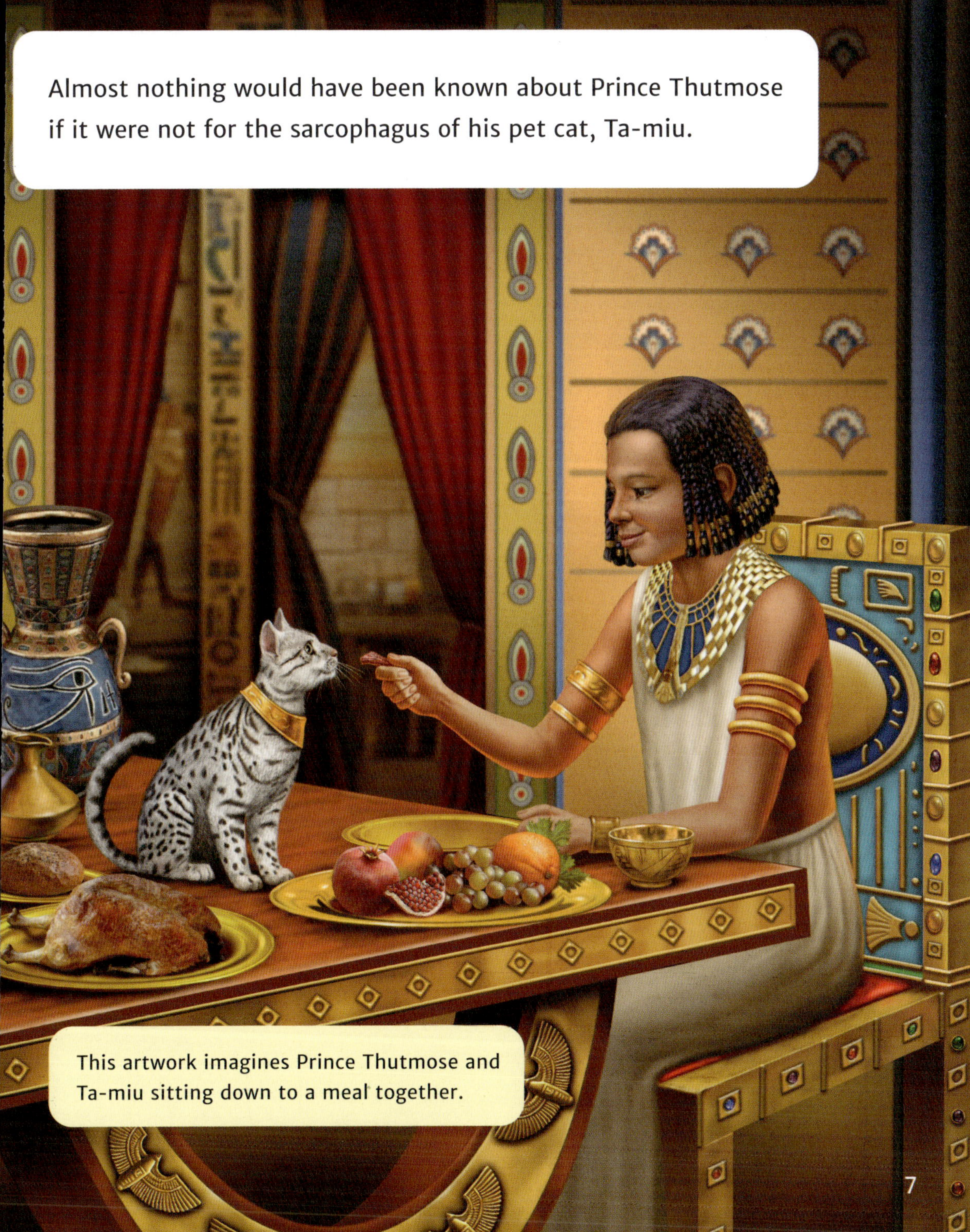

This artwork imagines Prince Thutmose and Ta-miu sitting down to a meal together.

Félicette – The First Cat in Space

Many different animals have been sent into space: dogs, rats, chimpanzees and monkeys, to name just a few. But Félicette (pronounced *feh-lee-set*) is the only cat to travel into space and return safely.

In 1963, French scientists trained 14 cats for space flight. They wanted to study the effects of space flight on the cats' brains and hearts. Félicette was one of them.

Félicette's photo with a paw print signature became famous after her journey.

Félicette had been a stray, living on the streets of Paris, before a pet dealer collected her with 13 other cats and sold them to the scientists. She was given the number C341 and put into a two-month training program with the other cats. They learnt to live in small containers and to become **accustomed** to the noise of rockets.

In their astronaut training, the cats became used to the amount of room they would have in the small rocket and had their brain activity measured using implants.

As the launch day for the space flight drew near, C341 was chosen from the 14 cats to be the first cat in space. She was selected for her calm nature. C341 was launched into space on 18 October 1963 from a site in Algeria. The flight lasted for 13 minutes and went 157 kilometres into the air. C341's heart rate, breathing and brain activity were **monitored** during the rocket's **ascent**, its five minutes of weightlessness and its re-entry. A parachute lowered the spaceship's capsule back to Earth, with C341 safely inside.

Félicette's capsule was launched into space on top of a small rocket.

The equipment that Félicette used was later shown during a 1964 exhibition, modelled by another cat.

The media were very interested in the cat that went to space, and named C341 “Félix”, after a cartoon character. When they realised that this Félix was actually female, her name was changed to Félicette.

France continued its space program, but they began to use monkeys instead of cats. So, Félicette remains the only cat to travel into space and back.

Today, there is a statue of Félicette at the International Space University in Strasbourg, France.

Félicette’s journey to space will always be remembered.

News of Félicette’s trip spread quickly around the world.

Space cat back alive

PARIS, Saturday. — France has successfully sent a cat into space on board a Veronique rocket and brought it back to earth alive.

An Armed Forces Ministry communique said the flight was carried out from Hammaguir base in the Sahara.

The cat came down by parachute.

The cat-in-space experiment was part of France's program of space biology research in which three rats have already been sent aloft.

Electrodes fitted to the

First French space shots with rats were to find the effects of absence of gravity on an animal's nervous system and brain activity. These effects were found to be small.

By using a cat, the scientists were able to analyse an animal's reactions more thoroughly and use a very delicate neuro-physiological technique so far achieved only in a laboratory.

The Grumpiest Cat on the Internet

Nobody ever expected Tardar Sauce, an ordinary mixed-breed cat, to become a social media celebrity. The little cat became famous in 2012, when her owner's brother thought that her "grumpy" expression was amusing and uploaded a photo of her to a social media website. Grumpy Cat went viral. Other people used her image to create more posts. By 2019, Grumpy Cat had millions of likes and followers on social media platforms.

Grumpy Cat became famous around the world for how she looked.

Grumpy Cat appeared on TV shows like *American Idol*.

Tardar Sauce's famous grumpy expression was caused by an underbite in her teeth and by being undersized. But despite always looking **disgruntled**, her owner said that most of the time, she was just a regular cat.

But this regular cat made many appearances on television and in commercials for cat food and cereal. She flew first class in planes, slept in a private hotel room with a king-sized bed, and had a personal assistant and a chauffeur. There were Grumpy Cat books, t-shirts, stuffed toys, wall calendars, a Grumppuccino iced coffee drink, a film and a video game.

Grumpy Cat's book "celebrates the grouch in all of us".

What did Grumpy Cat think of all of this? Like the title of her video game, she appeared to be *Grumpy Cat: Unimpressed*.

Ernest Hemingway's Polydactyl Cats

Some people collect postage stamps. Some collect coins. The famous American writer Ernest Hemingway cared for a lot of cats – six-toed cats.

Most cats have five toes on their front feet and four on their back feet. Hemingway's cats were **polydactyl** cats. They carried a **gene** that resulted in cats with additional toes, usually six but sometimes more. Polydactyl is a word taken from a Greek word that means "many fingers".

Polydactyl paws are harmless to a cat's health and are most often found on front paws.

Ernest Hemingway cradles one of his many cats at his home in San Francisco de Paula, Cuba.

In the 1930s, Ernest Hemingway had a house on Key West, a small island in the south of the state of Florida, USA. Hemingway was fond of sailing, and he met a sea captain who gave him a white, six-toed kitten. Some sailors believe that six-toed cats bring good luck to ships.

Hemingway took the white kitten home and named her Snow White. Snow White bred with local cats, and her kittens often had six toes. Hemingway didn't seem to mind how many kittens arrived. "One cat just leads to another," he said. By the time Hemingway died in 1961, it is said that he had owned about 200 cats.

Ernest Hemingway and two of his sons, Patrick and Gregory, play with kittens.

Hemingway's house is now a museum of his life and work, and it is still home to polydactyl cats. There are usually around 60 at the house: cats of all colours, shapes, sizes and personalities. About half have extra toes. They are named after famous people from Hemingway's time, including the aviator Amelia Earheart and the actors Cary Grant and Marilyn Monroe. A vet visits once a week to check on the cats' health.

Hemingway House employees can identify the different cats by name for visitors, and point out their favourite spots around the property.

Some of the cats still sleep on Hemingway's old bed, and they all roam freely around the house.

In 2017, a hurricane was forecast – Hurricane Irma. Everybody was advised to **evacuate** from the island that Hemingway House is on. When the museum employees tried to round up the cats to take them inside, they found the cats were clearly aware of the coming storm, because many had already come in. Ten employees volunteered to stay to look after the cats and, with 54 cats, they remained on the island throughout the storm. They made it through with no loss of life or injury – to humans or cats.

Royal Dogs

When a seven-year-old girl was given a corgi puppy in 1933, she loved it so much that she kept corgis for the rest of her life. That puppy was named Dookie, and the girl was Her Royal Highness Princess Elizabeth of York, who became Her Majesty Queen Elizabeth II. Dookie was the first of more than 30 corgis and dorgis (a cross between a corgi and a dachshund) that the Queen owned over close to 90 years.

The young Princess Elizabeth hugs her family's pet corgis Jane and Dookie in London, 1936.

The Queen's many dogs had a wide range of names, including Honey, Brush, Tinker and Sweep.

Queen Elizabeth was known to walk her dogs every day, as in this photo with her husband, Prince Philip, at Windsor Castle in 1959.

The royal dogs enjoyed a life of luxury. They had their own special rooms in the Queen's palaces. Their baskets were placed above the floor to keep draughts off them while they were sleeping. They also had a personal chef to prepare their meals of beef, lamb, chicken and rabbit.

The corgis were not always well behaved. They sometimes nipped at staff and visitors. One bit a soldier, a member of the Queen's Guard; another bit a postal worker delivering mail to Balmoral Castle in Scotland. Even the Queen was bitten once, as she unwisely tried to break up a fight between two dogs.

A Queen's Guard stands outside Buckingham Palace.

Never intervene in a dog fight. It is very dangerous – even if the dogs are familiar to you.

Queen Elizabeth regularly walked her many beloved corgis and dorgis.

When the Queen died in 2022, her final two corgis, Muick and Sandy, waited to say goodbye to her as her funeral procession reached Windsor Castle.

When Muick and Sandy themselves finally die, they will be taken to a special cemetery on the Queen's former **estate** at Sandringham in Norfolk, England. There, they will be buried alongside every other English royal pet that has died since Queen Victoria's collie Noble in 1887.

The Queen's last two corgis, Muick and Sandy, wait to farewell the Queen at Windsor Castle after her death.

Two Loyal Dogs

Some dogs become so attached to their owners that they will never leave them.

Greyfriars Bobby

A small Skye terrier, who became known as Greyfriars Bobby, lived in Edinburgh, Scotland, in the mid-nineteenth century. His master was a night **watchman** for the Edinburgh police named John Gray. Bobby accompanied John Gray on his patrol every night, following him through the dark, winding streets and alleys. They were the best of companions.

Then, in 1858, John Gray died. He was buried in the grounds of an old church called Greyfriars **Kirk**. Bobby was at the funeral. But, when the funeral was over and everyone left, Bobby didn't. He refused to leave his master's grave, and he stayed in the **kirkyard**, day after day, even in the worst weather.

Visitors can still go to Greyfriars Kirk.

This memorial statue of Greyfriars Bobby stands in the grounds of Greyfriars Kirk.

Bobby became famous in Edinburgh. People would gather to watch him as he left the kirkyard for the only time he came out each day. At one o'clock, Bobby would go to the coffee house that he had regularly been to with his master. He was given a meal there.

Bobby kept his loyal watch over John Gray's grave for 14 years, until he died himself in 1872.

Today, a statue of Bobby stands in Greyfriars kirkyard.

Hachikō

Hachikō (pronounced *hah-chee-koh*) was the pet dog of Hidesaburō Ueno, a professor at the University of Tokyo in Japan, in 1924. Professor Ueno lived in Shibuya, Tokyo, and every morning he travelled to his teaching job at the university on the train from Shibuya Station. In the evening, he returned.

Professor Ueno taught Agriculture at the University of Tokyo.

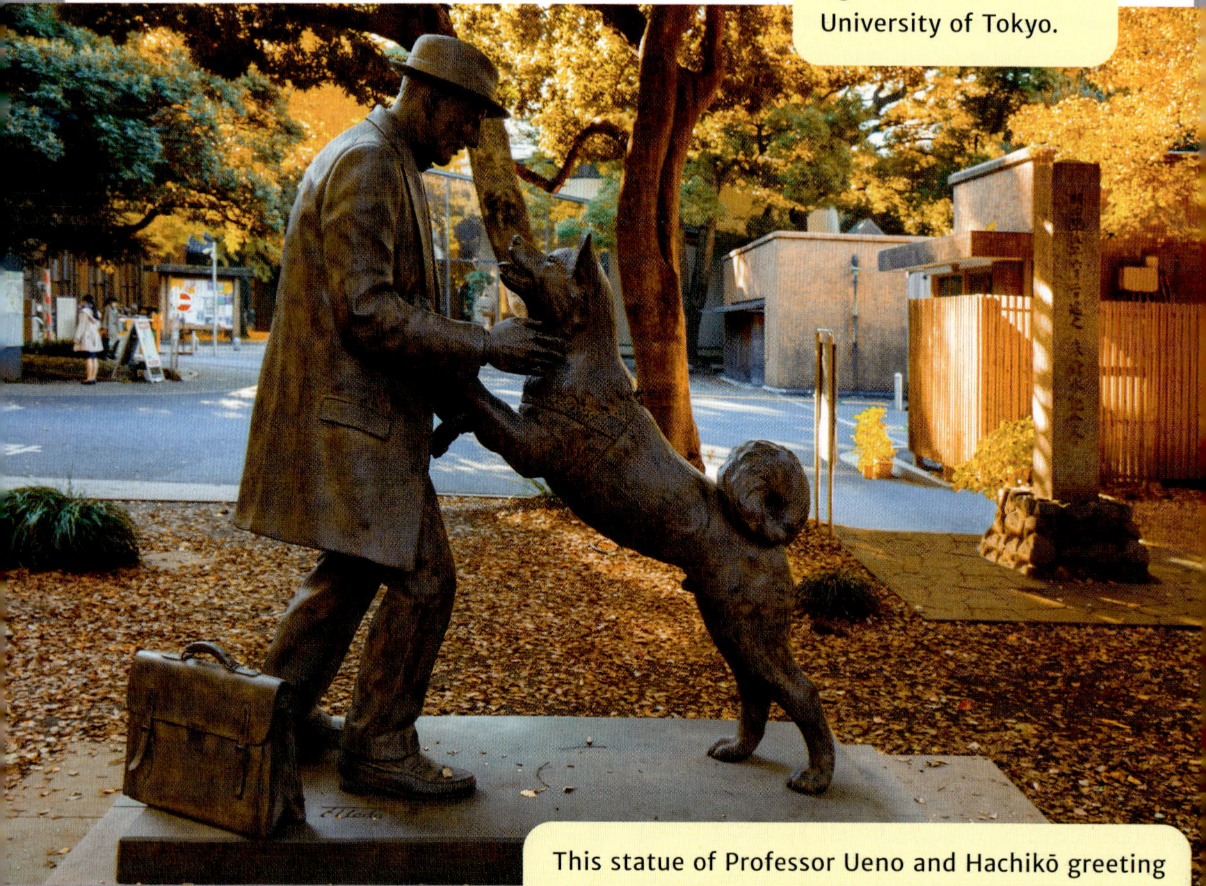

This statue of Professor Ueno and Hachikō greeting each other was installed at the University of Tokyo.

Every evening, Hachikō would be at the station waiting for him. No one took Hachikō to the station. Somehow, he knew exactly when the train was due and he would be waiting, precisely on time. People who used Shibuya Station became accustomed to seeing Hachikō come to meet his master.

Then, one day in 1925, Professor Ueno did not arrive on his usual train. He had been taken ill at work and had died suddenly. He would never come home on that train again.

That did not stop Hachikō. Every day, he continued to go to the station at the usual time. Surely one day, his master would come home!

Hachikō waits for Professor Ueno at Shibuya train station.

People began to notice Hachikō. They gave him food. One of Professor Ueno's former students, Hirokichi Saito, wrote an article about the faithful dog. It was published, and Hachikō became famous. He was seen as a symbol of loyalty and faithfulness.

When people realised that Hachikō was still waiting for Professor Ueno, they began to feed him and care for him.

Students pose beside the statue of Hachikō in Shibuya.

When Hachikō died in March 1935, he was buried next to his beloved master. Now, every year in April, hundreds of people gather at Shibuya Station for a ceremony that remembers Hachikō, the dog that waited.

Lassie – The Dogs Behind the Star

Lassie is one of the best-known dogs in the world. She was a fictional female collie and the main character of the 1943 feature film, *Lassie Come Home*. The film was a hit, and Lassie starred again in further films. A television series followed, and then more films and a TV series. In 2005, there was a remake of the original *Lassie Come Home* film called *Lassie*, so, Lassie was a very busy girl.

Except that "Lassie" wasn't a girl at all. And she wasn't just one dog. Nobody is quite sure just how many different dogs have played Lassie over the years, but there have been at least nine. And every one of them was male. Male dogs were chosen because they were bigger and had thicker coats throughout the year.

The actor Elizabeth Taylor hugs the dog Pal, playing Lassie, in the film *Lassie Come Home* (1943).

The first Lassie was a dog named Pal. When the film was being made, several collies were auditioned for the lead role and as **understudies**. Pal didn't get the starring role; he was to be an understudy. But then, during filming, the dog chosen as the lead refused to do a scene where Lassie had to swim across a river. Pal happily swam the river – and became the star.

When Pal retired, his descendants were chosen to play the part of Lassie. Pal's grandson, a collie named Baby, played the Lassie role for the longest time: six years.

Today, Lassie has her own star on the Hollywood Walk of Fame in Los Angeles.

Lassie is one of only three animals to have a star on the Hollywood Walk of Fame. The others are also dogs: Rin-Tin-Tin and Strongheart (both German shepherds).

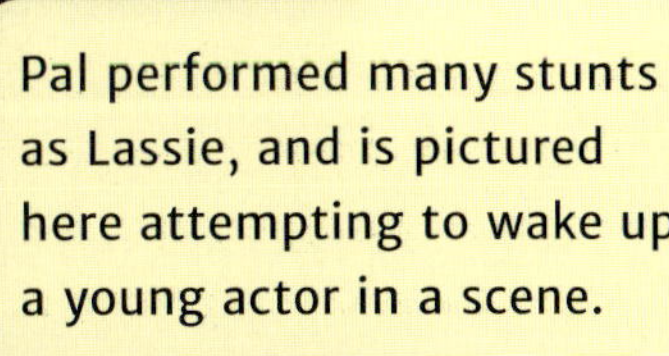

Pal performed many stunts as Lassie, and is pictured here attempting to wake up a young actor in a scene.

From very early times, cats and dogs have lived together with humans. Sometimes, they work together. Sometimes, they just keep each other company. And sometimes, cats and dogs have amazed humans with their courage, lovable personalities, loyalty and star quality.

Dog actor Uggie the Jack Russell Terrier poses with the Best Picture award for the film *The Artist* at the Golden Globe Awards in 2012.

One of Pal's descendants, Howard, poses with a camera while starring in the 1994 film *Lassie*.

Glossary

accustomed (*adjective*) used to or familiar with something

afterlife (*noun*) a life that some people believe exists after death

ancestor (*noun*) a family member who lived a long time ago

ascent (*noun*) a climb or rise upwards

descendants (*noun*) family members born many years later

disgruntled (*adjective*) grumpy, annoyed

estate (*noun*) a large property, usually in the country, that is owned by one person or family

evacuate (*verb*) to leave a dangerous area

gene (*noun*) part of a cell that passes a quality on from a parent to a child

grieving (*verb*) mourning a loss

hieroglyphs (*noun*) symbols used in ancient Egyptian writing

kirk (*noun*) a Scottish church

kirkyard (*noun*) an area of land around a Scottish church, which is often also a graveyard

monitored (*verb*) watched carefully over a period of time

nomadic (*adjective*) moving from place to place

pharaoh (*noun*) a king of ancient Egypt

polydactyl (*adjective*) having more than the usual number of fingers or toes

sacred (*adjective*) important and highly respected within religious beliefs

sarcophagus (*noun*) a stone coffin used in ancient times

understudies (*noun*) performers who replace other performers when they are unable to appear

watchman (*noun*) in the past, a member of the police who patrolled the streets of a town

Index

Baby 29
Balmoral Castle 20
Dookie 18
Edinburgh 22, 23
Egypt 3, 4, 6, 31
England 3, 21
Félicette/C341 8–11
films 13, 28, 29, 30
France 8, 11
Gray, John 22, 23
Greyfriars Bobby 22–23
Grumpy Cat/Tardar Sauce 12–13
Hachikō 24–27
Hemingway, Ernest 14–17
Hollywood Walk of Fame 29
Hurricane Irma 17
Japan 24
Key West 15
kirkyard 22, 23, 31
Lassie 28–29, 30
Pal 28, 29, 30
pets 3, 4, 5, 7, 9, 18, 21, 24
Prince Thutmose 4, 5, 6, 7
Queen Elizabeth II 18–21
sarcophagus 4, 5, 6, 7, 32
scientists 8, 9
Scotland 20, 22
Shibuya 24, 25, 27
Snow White 15
social media 12
space 3, 8, 10, 11
statues 4, 6, 11, 23, 24, 27
Ta-miu 4–7
Ueno, Hidesaburō 24, 25, 26
USA 14, 15
Windsor Castle 19, 21